COLLECTOR OF THINGS
& OTHER POEMS

Written by
Riya Aarini

Illustrated by
Valentina Serrano

Collector of Things & Other Poems
Text copyright © 2021 by Riya Aarini
Illustrations by Valentina Serrano

Publisher's Cataloging-in-Publication Data

Names: Aarini, Riya, author. | Serrano, Valentina, illustrator.
Title: Collector of things & other poems / written by Riya Aarini ; illustrated by
    Valentina Serrano.
Description: Chicago, IL : Riya Aarini, 2021.| Includes 126 b&w illustrations. | Includes
    index. | Audience: Ages 8-10. | Summary: A collection of light verse for children.
Identifiers: LCCN 2021902741 | ISBN 9781735347394 (pbk.) | ISBN 9781736316900
    (hardcover) | ISBN 9781736316917 (ebook)
Subjects: LCSH: Children's poetry, American. | Humorous poetry—Juvenile literature.|
    BISAC: JUVENILE FICTION / General. | JUVENILE FICTION / Poetry.
Classification: LCC PZ7.1 A2 C6 2021 | DDC J 811 A--dc22
LC record available at https://lccn.loc.gov/2021902741

Library of Congress Control Number: 2021902741

Visit www.riyapresents.com

To R.S.

Thanks for the bag of air. I still have it!

Half Undone

Mr. Finney Finnegan
Would always begin again.
He'd never finish what he'd begun.
He was the most interesting craftsman under the sun.
He'd start out right and end up wrong,
Because what he did, he left half undone!
He started building a wooden chair,
But it couldn't be used anywhere.
Instead of four legs to seat Emmy Lou,
The chair ended up with only two!

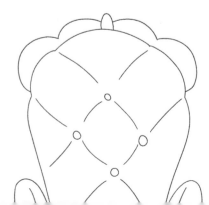

Contagious

Kindness is contagious.
Laughter is, too.
They're the only two things
I'm willing to catch from you!

Glass Half Full

Is the glass half empty?
Or is the glass half full?
What if you poured juice in?
Would it make it more full or less empty?
What if you drank it up?
Would it make it more empty or less full?
Full or empty, I'm so confused.
I just want a glass of juice!

Everyone's to Blame

When Matthew didn't put away his toy, Mom asked why.
This was Matthew's lively reply:
"I didn't put away my choo-choo train
Because the weatherman said it would rain.
And because it was dark and drizzly,
The great big ship got lost at sea.
The grumpy old captain forgot his way,
And a pirate stole the ship and steered it to the bay.
The pirate kidnapped the train conductor off the ground.
The conductor couldn't make the train's choo-choo sound.
I didn't hear the choo-choo, so I didn't wake from my nap.
All this happened in the afternoon and that was that.
The conductor, pirate, captain, weatherman, and rain
Are why I didn't put away my choo-choo train.
So, you see, everyone else is to blame . . .
except me!"

9

Laughing Sickness

I laughed so hard I buckled!
My eyes got teary.
I sniffled and I snuffled.
My sight grew bleary.
My tummy shook!
I grabbed my achy belly.
It really hurt!
I bowled over, really!
This is what to expect
When you get a laughing sickness!

Questions

Questions, schmestions!
So many questions!
How are you?
What's two plus two?
Questions, questions, everywhere!
Hey, you! What are you doing there?
Do you have the time?
Have you got a dime?
Questions, questions, what do I do?
Oh, no! Now I'm asking questions, too!

Movie Genres

The life of daredevil Neville is an action-packed thriller.
His life goes by so fast, it's one crazy blur!
Danny and Leigh are lovey-dovey.
Their lives are a romantic comedy!
Shhh! Annabelle lives secretly.
Her life is a cozy mystery!
Lee and Bee fight, and no one knows what for.
Their lives are an animated war!
What genre does your life fit in?
Well, your movie script is still being written!

Adding to the World

Jokester Jan put a joke into the world,
Laughter we didn't have before.
Doodling Dan put a drawing into the world,
Inspiration we hadn't felt before.
Singing Sally put a song into the world,
Music we hadn't heard before.
But what did *you* put into the world,
That wasn't there before?

The Bigalaboo

Mr. McGoo told me of the Bigalaboo.
He said it's big and furry and smelly, too!
I looked at him with suspicion.
But I continued to listen.
He said it's got claws and teeth and warts.
The monster has purple spots of all sorts!
It comes out at night when you're asleep
And tickles your toes and goes *bippety beep!*
"Is that all?" I asked Mr. McGoo.
He asked, "Doesn't that frighten you?"
I said, "I laugh when something tickles my toes.
It sounds pretty neat, as far as a monster goes."
"You're quite a brave little boy," replied Mr. McGoo.
"I don't know anyone who's unafraid of the Bigalaboo!"
I stayed wide awake that night,
Hoping to see this monstrous sight.
But the Bigalaboo never came.
The night was just the same.
It was dark and quiet,
And I grew tired.
Soon I fell fast asleep,
Without a Bigalaboo to tickle my feet!

Marge in Charge

Freckled-faced Marge
Liked to be in charge.
She was only three feet tall
But had the might of a cannonball.
At just five years old,
Her orders were bold.
She'd tell Bob what to say
And Mary where to play.
If eager Marge could,
She'd tell where the raindrops should
Fall on a rainy day!

Conversations

I tell Sally that I drank a fizzy root beer.
Sally tells Will that one crazy day I rode a deer.
Will tells Kim that my dear uncle lives on the frontier.
Kim tells Becky that my gramps was a pioneer.
Becky tells Sam that I'm leaving after the school year.
To my friends, all this is crystal clear.

By the time it gets back to me, I hear . . .
I have a future career as a mountaineer,
That I'm on the lookout for hiking gear,
And at the zoo, I'm an animal volunteer!
It seems I'm having a really good year . . .
When all I did was have a root beer!

Holding Mom's Hand

My mom wants me to hold her hand always.
Otherwise, she'll get lost, she says.
It's a really big world out there,
And my mom needs my care.
I'll hold her hand so she doesn't trip or fall.
I'll hold Mom's hand so she won't get lost at all.

Millionaire Montgomery

Montgomery Faire
Was the worst kind of millionaire.
He had a million hairs on his head.
He had a million dust balls under his bed.
He'd done a million itty bitty wrongs.
He'd sung a million old country songs.
As for money, Millionaire Montgomery
Didn't have one penny!

Baker Mixitup

I stepped into Baker Mixitup's kitchen.
At once, my senses were smitten!
I saw mounds of treats galore,
And foods I'd never seen before!
In the oven baked garlic pie.
I had a whiff, and, oh my!
His pasta was covered in chips,
Semisweet chocolate, that is!
There was a tower of cream puffs
Filled with greenish pea stuff!
On his shelf sat salmon pralines
And buttercream-frosted lima beans!
I tried a sample of each delight.
Every concoction tasted just right.
Baker Mixitup prepares the finest fare.
Just try his silly creations, if you dare!

Just Right

If you sneeze once, it's *gesundheit!*
If you sneeze a lot, they'll stay out of sight.
If you laugh once, it's fun.
It's weird if you laugh for no reason.
If you cry once, you'll get a hug.
If you cry too much, it's swept under the rug.
In the world, you'll be all right,
When you sneeze, laugh, and cry just right.

Dreaming

I fell asleep and soon was dreaming.
I was on a pirate ship—I'd have you believing.
I was stuck somewhere at sea,
Surrounded by pirates, at least twenty.
They tied me to the ship's mast.
The pirate ship sailed onward fast.
I got loose and ran free, or so I thought.
But soon enough, once more, I was caught.
And so, it went on and on again.
Aye, the pirates were gritty men!
By the end of the chase and capture,
I found myself in bed in a rapture.
Still, all that running was rough.
Now I'm too tired to wake up!

I Lost My Head!

I lost my head!
I don't know where it went!
I got mad and my face turned red.
Next thing I knew, I lost my head!
I've got to find it really soon,
'Cause I can't sing a single tune!
I can't eat a thing, not one nibble,
Without my head at the dinner table.
I must find it before bed.
I won't sleep without my head!
Today is the worst day that's ever been.
I never want to lose my head again.

Chocolate Sea

If there's one place May wanted to be,
It was over the hills and beyond the oak tree—
A truly wonderous place with a chocolate sea.

Melted chocolate filled the glen evermore.
Waves of chocolate pounded the shore.
May could hear the chocolate sea roar!

There floated truffles and chocolates milk and dark.
Each bonbon was printed with a special mark.
In the surf drifted chocolate peppermint bark!

May dreamed of swimming in the chocolate sea.
She'd float and soak and be all chocolatey.
'Til May gets her chocolate sea, maybe she'll agree
. . . to settle for this box of plain ol' chocolate candy!

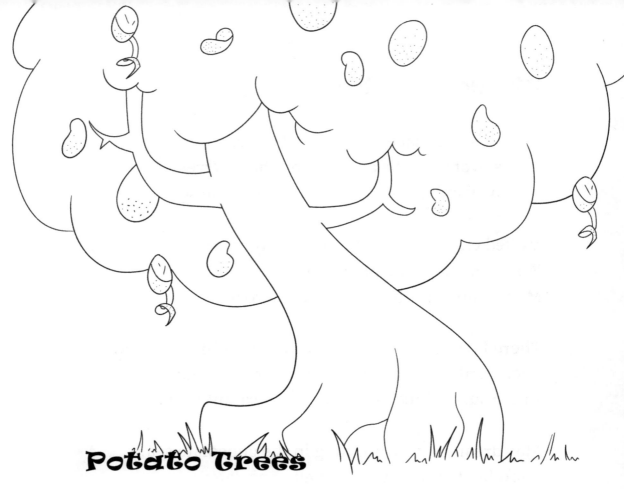

Potato Trees

What if potatoes grew on trees?
Would they grow in bunches of twos or threes?
Would the tiny flower buds
Grow into big, round spuds?
When the sun shines in the meadows,
Would the tree grow roasted potatoes?
Or would they be crisp as potato chips?
And would the neighbors lick their lips?
If they squashed the spuds under their feet,
Would we have mashed potatoes to eat?
Potato trees are a wonder.
I'm just glad the spuds grow under . . . the ground!

26

A Chance of Peas Showers

What if, one day, you heard the weatherman say,
Tomorrow, we'll have peas showers all day.
The raining green peas would be like slush.
The streets would be covered in pea mush.
The weather would never be the same again,
If we had green peas falling as rain!
There might be a slight chance of peas in the forecast.
So, if you're out and about, better hurry home fast!
With mushy peas falling, we might need galoshes.
I'm just glad it doesn't rain cold sausage!

The Thingamajig

Mrs. Brig told me about the Thingamajig.
It's soft and cuddly and really big!
She said it bakes cookies and cake.
There's nothing a Thingamajig can't make.
It puts on an apron over its blue fur
To keep away splashes when it stirs!
But the Thingamajig can only be seen
When it's dark and the kitchen is clean.
The monster won't bake in a messy place.
In fact, it won't even show its face!
So, if you want to see the Thingamajig at all,
You better clean the plates and wash the hall.
Then you might hear a rattle in the kitchen.
Shhh! Stay in bed and quietly listen.
You'll hear the *cling-clang!* of pots and pans
And *dings!* of bowls in the Thingamajig's hands.
The whirring of mixers might keep you awake.
But don't bother the monster, for goodness' sake!
By morning you'll smell breakfast cake,
Made by a Thingamajig that loves to bake.

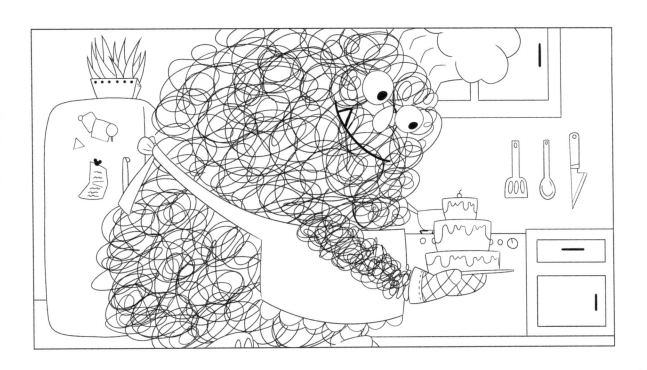

Don't Judge

Please don't judge little Sally Ryder . . .
For being a nervous nail biter.
Please don't judge Oklahoma state . . .
For joining the union late.
Please don't judge the shoe factory . . .
For making tying laces hard as can be.
Please don't judge Mississippi . . .
For being too long to spell properly.
And please don't judge Baker Frontz . . .
For baking broccoli into his croissants!

Mustache Man

Señor Robero wears a sombrero.
He sells mustaches on the street.
He's the most mustache-y man you'll ever meet.
He sells mustaches for the bull fight.
These are twirled at the ends just right.
He sells mustaches for the motorcycle ride.
They stay put when cruising side by side.
He sells mustaches for concerts in the park,
And those that light up after dark.
His mustaches are the best in town.
They hide even the most slinking frown.
If you smile a lot, you won't need his wares.
Just remember him when you've got many cares.

Sweet Deal

Sweet-toothed Lou wanted to make a deal.
He'd get candy for every single meal.
In return, he'd eat everything on his plate.
Sweet Lou wouldn't let one bit go to waste.
For breakfast, he'd have licorice and lemon drops.
He'd finish it off with gummy bears and lollipops.
At lunch, he'd start with cotton candy,
And end with bubble gum and taffy.
Dinner would be a twenty-piece box
Of chocolate bars and sugar rocks.
The sad thing is, for sweet Lou,
Of course, his deal didn't go through!

Saving for a Rainy Day

I'm saving for a rainy day.
It seems the sun is expectin' me to pay.
I have to figure out how much it'll cost
To get back the sunshine that we lost.
A penny, nickel, or dime, I say,
How much is it for one sun's ray?

Boring Cousin Bill

My cousin crunches cranberry chips.
He double dunks Danishes in dips.
He chills cabbage soup at the coffee shop,
And licks his Lebanese lollipop.
Now no one will eat with him.
His tastes are too plain for us.
Our family's the risk-taking kind.
So, we left boring Bill behind!

Sleeping Foot

My left foot fell asleep.
I set the alarm for three o'clock.
On time, it went *beep, beep,*
But my foot stayed asleep in my sock.
So, I made it coffee in a cup.
Still, my foot wouldn't wake up.
My foot must have been dreaming,
Since toes were wriggling for goodness' sake!
Alarms and coffee weren't working.
I finally shook my foot wide awake.
It took time to shuffle around again.
It was better than what it had been.
One sleeping foot does me no good.
Two sleeping feet are far worse.
With one foot asleep, at least I stood.
But two sleeping feet are a curse!

Country Twang

Farmer Flynn Fang
Speaks with a country twang.
Just hearing him talk
Puts a pep in your walk!
The way he says each word,
Is like something you've never heard!
He makes "team" and "ring"
Sound like the same thing.
To him "gone" and "alone"
Have the same tone.
It's amazing how words can sound
When you're from a different part of town!

One of Me

There's only one you and only one me.
But what if there were ten, twelve, or twenty?
We'd each be our own baseball team.
(It would be one heck of a meme!)
I'd play shortstop, first base, and pitcher, too.
You'd do the same. It'd be me against you!
Just Ted, Paul, and Pam would fill the stands.
It'd be thirty of our friends as our fans!
But then again, from noon until three,
I'd have to share my toys with all ten of me.
Hmmm! That doesn't sound right!
Me, me, me, and me would fight.
That's not the way it should be.
I'm glad it's just one of you and one of me!

37

Forgetting

I reminded me.
He reminded she.
We reminded he.
She reminded thee.
We reminded each other a whole lot.
But in the end, we all forgot!

Brussels Sprouts

I wrote an angry letter
To my town's local paper.
I sent my letter to Editor Outs,
Complaining about Brussels sprouts.
I wrote that my mom couldn't buy them,
If the grocery stores wouldn't sell them.
Editor Outs wrote back by lunch.
He wrote that he had a hunch.
If my mom were anything like his,
She'd grow Brussels sprouts in her garden
And still feed them to the kids!

Borrowing from the Weather

Sally is over the moon.
Greg chases rainbows.
Jen gets wind of it too soon.
Jim hasn't the foggiest idea.
Bill and Rob shoot the breeze.
Frankie takes a shine to Maria.
I am right as rain when I tease . . .
Oh, the things we borrow from the weather
To say the darndest things to each other!

Long Underwear

Benny Blare always wears long underwear.
He wears them just about everywhere.
They're snug and comfy as can be.
They fit him really well, you see.
He wears his long underwear while shopping.
He wears them while cleaning and while mopping.
He wears them in the car and when out camping.
He wears them to the ballroom and while dancing.
Benny Blare loves his long underwear.
Try to understand, but please don't stare!

Elephant in the Classroom

There was an elephant in the classroom.
It wore a huge polka-dotted costume.
As the teacher taught math up front,
The elephant listened and gave a grunt.
No one paid attention to the schooling.
We all watched the elephant drooling.
Strangely, not one of us said a single word
About the elephant that we all saw and heard.

43

New Shoes

I got new shoes but they're stiff and tight.
I can't get my new shoes to feel just right.
They pinch right here and feel tight there.
I just hate walking anywhere!
I don't know for how much they sold,
But I can't wait for my new shoes to get old!

Robots

Robots do everything.
They pick up the recycling and trash,
Make a meal of corned beef and hash,
Vacuum and scrub the floors,
Drive the big, yellow tractors,
Pull the weeds,
Plant the seeds,
Write reports and plow the snow.
I just wish robots would do my homework, though.

Everyone's Famous

'Seems everyone is famous,
From Jen to Billy to Amos,
From cool YouTube stars
To drivers of racing cars,
From people on the news
To trios singing the blues.
Everyone is in a photo somewhere,
From billionaires to that one polar bear.
Every photo gets a hundred shares.
Now we all know the world's affairs!
Since everyone is famous to the bone,
I think it's more special to be unknown!

In the Thick of It

When I'm in the thick of it,
There's no end in sight.
When I'm out of it,
I'll be all right.

Mrs. Hurds

Good ol' Mrs. Hurds
Is a collector of words.
She carefully chooses every letter,
And turns it into something better.
What's absurd about Mrs. Hurds
Is her obsession with words.
She strings them together one by one.
Her threaded words give her endless fun!
She churns out sentences from the strings.
When they fit neatly on the page, she sings!
You hear her song three blocks away.
Those perfect pages make her day!
Then she gathers the pages into a book.
Before she ends, she takes one last look.
She climbs a ladder with book in hand
And places it in on a shelf so grand.
She's got eight hundred shelves so far, I think.
You wouldn't miss them, even if you blink.
She's too old to climb the ladder.
Day by day, it's getting sadder.
But she won't quit while she's got strength.
So onward she goes, adding books at length.
Her library towers so high, it's out of sight.
Books are stacked up, down, left, and right.

There's no room to walk.
And she will hardly talk.
She's got her nose in a book all day.
What more is there to say?

49

Freshly Made Bed

I've got a freshly made bed.
It's comfy and smells new.
Today, I think I'll sleep in.
Tomorrow, my bed will be stale.
I'll have to rewash the sheets,
So, I can snooze on again.

Blessed

Anna Marie Yest
Is incredibly blessed.
She's got feet on her toes
And a garden that grows.
She's got imagination in her head
And a dozen books that she's read.
She's got a tune that she whistles
And a few good jokes and riddles.
She's got a song to sing
And joy to bring.
Anna Marie's got everything!

Pretty Mary's Hair

Pretty Mary was pretty hairy.
She sang her hair a song so that it'd grow extra long.
She buttered her locks so they weren't rough as rocks.
Her hair was soft, not dry, and dripped with enough oil to fry!
Her hair sizzled under the sun like a crispy bun!
Mary showed lots of care to her silky hair.
And unlike other girls, Mary never cut her curls.
She lived in her hair, like it was her very own lair.
Pretty Mary wasn't scary, quite the contrary!
Being so hairy, Mary was cheerful as a canary.
Still, if you saw Mary's hair, you wouldn't be the first to stare!

Fine Line

It's a fine line between genius and insanity
Or an elephant and a manatee. . . .
One is big and round. The other is just the same.
Both eat green grass, and you never hear 'em complain.
Both mammals move as slow as can be.
But one walks on land; the other swims at sea!
As for genius and insanity, they're a complete mystery!

Fast Mr. Fritz

Mr. Fritz drove really fast.
He shifted gears and pressed the gas.
Going over the limit,
He sped like a bullet.
He drove everywhere in haste,
Thinking he had no time to waste.
He raced up the hills and in the towns below.
But there was one thing Mr. Fritz didn't know.
No matter how fast or slow he drove,
Whether from Red City to Palm Grove,
Or from Sinclair to Jefferson Square,
That place would still be there!

Grandpa Mel's Nose

My Grandpa Mel
Has a strong sense of smell,
And it's kept him very well.
He won't eat an egg without thinking.
He'll smell it first, and if it's stinking,
He'll throw it out without blinking.
Grandpa Mel will sniff for rain
Whether he's in Portland or in Maine.
His nose is like a weather vane!
If he smells a downpour,
He'll stay dry indoors
And won't go out anymore.
Grandpa Mel's big, round nose
Certainly, and always, knows
That not everything goes.
With his special sniffing ability,
Grandpa Mel has proudly lived to be
A fine one hundred and three!

Growing

I'm growing . . .
I'm growing like a tree.
I'm afraid I won't stop
Until I'm ninety-three.
I've just turned seven.
Already,
I can stretch to heaven.
There's no real knowing
How tall I'll get.
But I'll keep growing.
If every year is like the last,
My guess is,
I'll reach a hundred inches fast!

Rebecca the Raccoon

Someone gave President Coolidge a pet.
It was the best presidential gift yet.
He fondly named the racoon Rebecca.
Was the critter a handful? You betcha!
The first lady put a leash around its neck
And took it for walks until sunset.
One day Rebecca got really mad.
She bit President Coolidge's hand.
So, she was sent right away to the local zoo!
Think twice about keeping a racoon, won't you?

Spaghetti, Spaghetti

Spaghetti, spaghetti,
There's more than plenty.
I'll spoon you a plateful, if you let me.
Spaghetti, spaghetti,
Now don't you forget me!
I'm seated at the end of a table for one hundred and twenty!

Fisherman Dan

Fisherman Dan braved the sea.
He was daring but chatty.
He didn't have great glory—
But could he tell a story!
Down in the chilly cabin,
He kept the tough crew laughin'.
The sea air was thick and damp,
So, they huddled under the lamp.
As Fisherman Dan told his tale,
The fishing boat wouldn't sail.
The swimming fish would stop.
Into the fishing net they'd hop
To listen to stories of old
That good Fisherman Dan told.

Shade Stand

Tommy Flay would sell the shade
Like it was old-fashioned lemonade.
He'd mix it up
And put it in a cup.
All kids, ladies, and gents
Could buy it for five cents.
As the sun beat down,
Lines formed all around.
News spread about what he had made.
Folks wanted his homemade shade.
See, Tommy built his shade stand under a tree.
So, once you bought it, you'd have it instantly!

Shoe Tree

Ms. Eloise grows her shoes on trees.
I haven't seen it, but it's what I believe.
Every day, Ms. Eloise wears a different pair,
Yellow, blue, magenta, and red,
Striped, green, and polka-dotted.
Ms. Eloise grows her shoes somewhere.
I've heard her speak of her shoe trees.
She says her shoes stay shiny and new.
She picks them whenever she wants to.
I wish I had a shoe tree like Ms. Eloise.
I'd water and trim my shoe tree,
So that it'd grow sneakers for me.

Chasin' Squirrels

A tree squirrel went a-hoppin'.
It sent the watchful dog a-chasin'
And the surprised woman after it a-runnin'.
A-hoppin', a-chasin', and a-runnin',
It's what happens when you see a squirrel a-comin'!

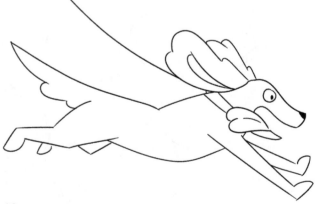

Bag of Air

Once, my brother gave me a bag of air.
He said it was the finest air in Delaware.
I opened the bag and breathed it in.
My heart sure raced and my head did spin.
I couldn't believe how fresh air could be.
I asked him if he'd mind going up to Tennessee.
There, I said, you'll find more luxuries,
Like pure air above its ancient, hidden seas.
He said he'd make the trip, but first
He needed to quench his dry thirst.
So, I handed him an empty drinking glass
Of the best invisible water from El Dorado Pass!

The Smiling Bug

The Bug grinned at me, said shy Emily.
It winked then blinked and tooted its horn!
Don't be silly, replied Billy Rae Thorn.
Cars don't make funny faces.
They only take you places.

Tea Kettle Whistle

I heard the tea kettle singing loud.
It was the sweetest whistling sound.
High-pitched and steady,
It meant the water was ready.
I'd soon have my hot cup of tea.
The thought warmed me up instantly.
Though it's a song I only hear once in a while,
The sound of the whistle sure makes me smile.

Nothing Lasts Forever

Life is strangely odd but clever.
You see, nothing lasts forever.
Not . . .
A gigantic sneeze
A fever of one-hundred degrees
Overgrown bangs and hunger pangs
Ice cream floats and spaghetti boats
Math homework and a sales perk
Or . . .
Laughs and cries and sweet potato pies
Always being last in line or that pesky library
fine
Arguments and compliments
Summer's heat and winter's shiver.
Quite rightly, nothing lasts forever.

Senses

The music sounds delicious.
The apple looks extra crisp.
The flowers smell nutritious.
The skunk feels like a lisp.
The blanket tastes soft.
I'm aware of what I've listed.
What have I forgot?
Huh? You think my senses are twisted?

A Very Bad Day

Today is a very bad day.
The clouds are gray,
And they won't go away.
My dog escaped his leash and collar.
All I could do was scream and holler.
I peeled an orange, and it tasted sour.
The minutes go by slower than the hour.
The temperature outside is freezing.
It's got me sniffling and sneezing.
I know that I'm not at all alone.
Some days are bad for everyone.
There's nothing left for me to say,
Except, *achoo!* It's been a very bad day.

Planting Happiness

I planted a seed of happiness
In the backyard garden plot.
I dug a hole and made a mess.
I hope my seed grows a lot.
I don't know when it will sprout
Or when it will start to bloom.
When it does, I sure won't pout.
And there'll be a lot less gloom.
Each day, I'll pluck a petal of happiness
And hold it gently in the palm of my hand.
Where it blooms next, I won't need to guess,
'Cause it'll be growing on my very own land!

70

Cookie Taster

I'd like a job in the cookie kitchen.
It's the cookies I want to be testin'.
I'll give the baked cookies a taste
And make sure none goes to waste.
On the counter the bowls will clatter,
As I watch the baker mix the batter.
When the cookies are pulled from the oven,
The whiff will send me to cookie heaven!
I'll make sure the cookies taste just right
Before anyone else takes a bite.
Sugar, peanut butter, chocolate, and cream,
Being a cookie taster is every kid's dream!

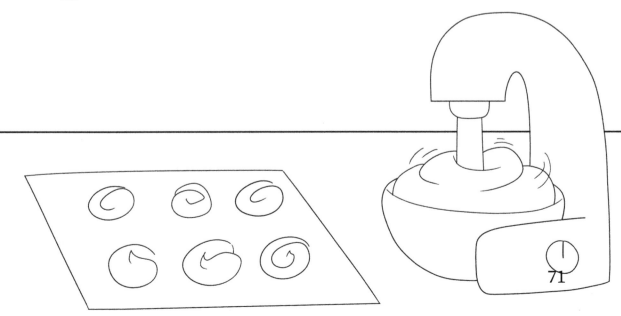

Gift Baskets

Why are gift baskets packed with pears
Wrapped in foil, then sold for a pretty penny,
When Dad can buy fruit from grocery stores
For under a dollar and get twice as many?

Work Phobic

Wilford was afraid of doing work.
He would grumble, shake his head, and shout.
The slightest bit of work made him pout.
Indeed, earning money was a perk.
But doing work made him complain.
He started charging customers double
So that he wouldn't have the trouble
Of ever doing any work again!

The News

My Auntie Lee is a news junkie.
She blares the news all day long.
If it's not the radio then it's the TV.
All I hear is what's going wrong.

The news rarely says what's right.
It's just crooks and television crews
Blasted all day and all night.
Why aren't kind deeds in the news?

I won't have all of these fears,
If the news is cheery once in a while.
I won't need to cover my ears,
If hearing the news makes me smile.

Raising Prices

Bo goes to the corner store.
He goes there all the time.
Everything he buys costs him a dime.
Then one day, the shop owner says,
"We've raised our prices, honey!"
Bo thought, *Do they think I'm made of money?*
From sticky buns to lollipops,
Everything costs a nickel more.
Now Bo no longer shops at the corner store!

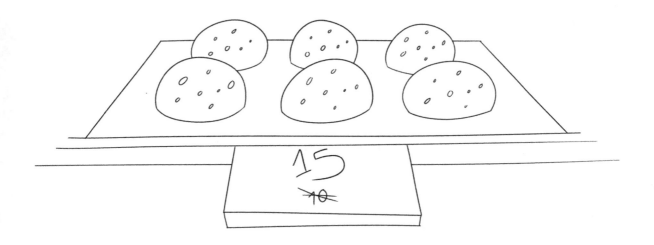

Stairs

Each morning Billy Bador
Takes the busy elevator
To avoid walking up three flights of stairs.
He comes home at six-fifteen
And steps on his stair machine
For two hours and still ends up right there!

Frugal Frank

Frugal Frank received a gift basket one night.
It was filled with thirty delicious delights,
From pears to chocolate-covered cherries,
And cheddar cheeses to logs of salamis.
It weighed twenty pounds and looked awfully nice.
But Frugal Frank thought about the price.
He gave it right back, 'cause he couldn't believe
It cost three months' worth of groceries!

Lost: MIND

Larry nailed up a sign
Saying he had lost his mind.
He had it earlier on,
But suddenly it was gone.
On the sign was written,
If anyone finds it, hold onto it,
And he'll come get it
In a New York minute.
It's not Larry's fault
That his mind got lost.
These days Larry feels so sad
Without the mind he once had.

Cake Paradise

Henry worked extra hours last week
So that he could buy a delicious treat.
It was chocolate cake with coffee cream.
It was every dessert lover's dream.
With his check he bought one slice.
The scrumptious cake tasted so nice!
He worked three hours overtime in snow and ice
For five minutes in cake paradise!

Lady Luck

Miss Lady Luck had a talk with me.
Our chat happened unexpectedly.
She asked if she might lend me some luck
So that in life, I wouldn't get stuck.
With a little luck, I'd win the lottery
And my pockets wouldn't be so empty.
With luck, I'd never be fed lima beans
Or eat caramel corn and get cavities.
With luck, I'd never have go to the dentist
Or get my name on Santa's naughty list.
Miss Lady Luck promised me lucky days.
But good luck comes in all sorts of ways.
I said, "Miss Lady Luck, I don't mean to be rude.
I'm already lucky because of my good attitude!"

Royal Pears

Some pears are royal
And wrapped in gold foil.
Surely, they're sweet,
But too kingly to eat!

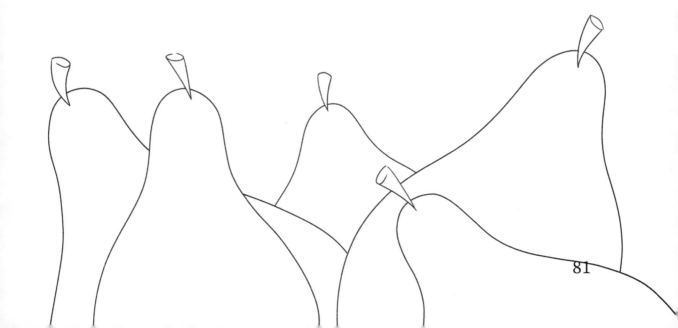

Symphony of Sounds

Uncle Greg makes musical sounds.
It happens when he moves around.
You'll hear a *pop!* a *click!* and a *crack!*
Coming from his knuckles, knees, and back.
Uncle Greg is his very own symphony,
But he says his tunes are terribly achy!

Being Sable

Sable asked, "Should I . . .
Think the unthinkable?
Accept the unacceptable?
Tolerate the intolerable?
Love the unlovable?
Befriend the unfriendable?
Question the unquestionable?
Answer the unanswerable?"
Auntie Anne replied, "Dear Sable,
Always do what you are able!"

Baby Vegetables

"I don't like vegetables," complained Emma Sue.

"I know," said Aunt Pam, "but some are grown just for you!

Small beets, turnips, and leeks are called baby vegetables,

And these mini delights are quite delectable.

Some folks are even baby vegetable professionals.

They know when they see an acceptable vegetable.

They've tasted beans and squash that are unforgettable!"

Emma Sue wanted to be respectable,

So, she asked for a side of baby vegetables.

She said, "I'll have some baby veggies, if you please."

And Aunt Pam gave her a helping of broccoli and peas.

Giggles

Melanie Biggle
Has got quite a giggle.
You can hear it from a block away.
Ed said something funny
About the bees and honey,
And she couldn't stop giggling all day.
She does an amusing wiggle
Whenever she gets a giggle.
She's a wiggling, giggling sunshine ray!

Plenty of Friends

Friends? Do I have any?
Sure, I've got many!
Jenny introduced me to Kenny.
Kenny brags to me about Benny.
Benny sent me a funny email from Penny.
(Penny once lent me grocery money.)
Penny went shopping with me and Lenny.
Lenny spent the twenty lent by Penny.
Lenny sings karaoke with Henry.
Henry, Lenny, Penny, Benny, Kenny, and Jenny.
Friends? I've got plenty!

At the Pet Store

Bobby went to the pet store.
He asked the clerk, "What do you do?"
"I sell fish."
"Oh, you selfish?"
"Yes, I sell fish."
"Why don't you give?"
"No, I don't give fish. I *sell* fish."
"What fish do you sell?"
"I sell goldfish, blowfish, and rockfish.
Would you like to buy a fish?"
Bobby replied, "No. I'm too selfish to have a pet."

Speedy, Squealy Tim

Speedy Tim thought the traffic lights had it in for him.
As soon as he sped, the stoplight turned red.
He came to a screeching halt, and it was all the light's fault.
His tires wore down, and his brakes squealed loud.
It was all because the stoplight had it in for Squealy Tim.

Owner Walking

I saw a dog a-walkin', its owner trailing far behind.
I guess it's fair to say that the doggy didn't mind.
The dog pulled forward with all its might.
It dragged its owner both left and right!
When the dog sat, the owner would stand.
It was clear who had the upper hand.
The dog was in charge of its owner.
Laughing, I bowled over!
I will never forget that spectacular day
I saw a dog walking its owner every which way!

Normal is Strange

Normal is quite unusual.
Who's to say who's normal or not normal?
Who's to say what normal is or was or will be?
What's normal yesterday may be odd today.
What's normal tomorrow may have been peculiar yesterday.
There's no telling who or what will be normal or when or why.
Normal is very strange indeed!

Punctuation Romance

Sammi and Colin got married.
They became known as *semicolon*.
When Colin divorced Sammi,
He went back to being *colon*.

Ettie and Al dated for a year.
The pair had met while working at charities.
Et is short for Ettie, we hear.
Now they're known as *et al* at universities.

Brittle Brandon

Brittle Brandon was unbendable as a lemon drop.
He was breakable as peanut brittle sold at the coffee shop.
He'd crumble at the slightest snub and crack after a snicker.
Brittle Brandon broke into pieces after a bicker.
Be careful around Brittle Brandon, since he can break.
Best be unlike Brittle Brandon and be soft as cake.

Bouncy Brittany

Bouncy Brittany was one-of-a-kind.
Whatever happened, she didn't mind.
Everything in the entire world
Bounced off this springy girl.
From mean sneers to horrid jeers,
Bouncy Brittany knew no fears.
She was soft and bendable as can be;
Every hurtful word bounced off easily.
Bouncy Brittany never broke a sweat.
She could teach us all how not to fret!

Never Satisfied

Peter Pied was never satisfied.
He told the truth and never lied.
"The day is bright!" Sue Ellen cried.
"I've had brighter," Peter replied.
"The apples are red!" said Jeter.
"I've seen redder," grumbled Peter.
"You're doing well!" said the doctor.
"I've been better," mumbled Peter.
Peter Pied always spoke his mind.
Maybe one day he'll be satisfied!

Lonely Crumb

Once there was a lonely crumb.
The lonely crumb was introduced to L.
Crumb and L happily came together as Crumble.
Then the duo Crumble was introduced to Cookie.
The trio joined forces to become Cookie Crumble.
Joyful Crumb was no longer lonely,
Since L and Cookie were good company.
But everyone loved a yummy cookie crumble.
Soon enough Cookie Crumble was gobbled up
Until Crumb was once again left lonely on the tabletop.

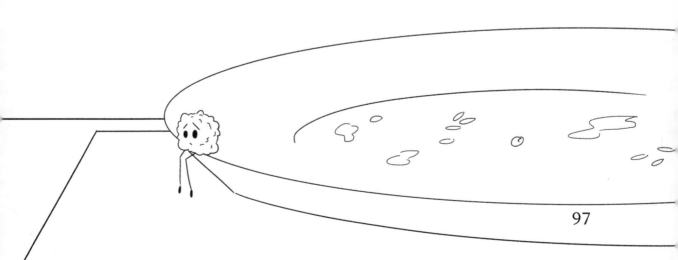

Norm and Al

Norm and Al were very good pals.
They were weird when apart.
But together they were NormAl.
Sometimes Ab, which is short for Abby,
Joined with Norm and Al to make three.
The unusual trio became AbNormAl, you see!

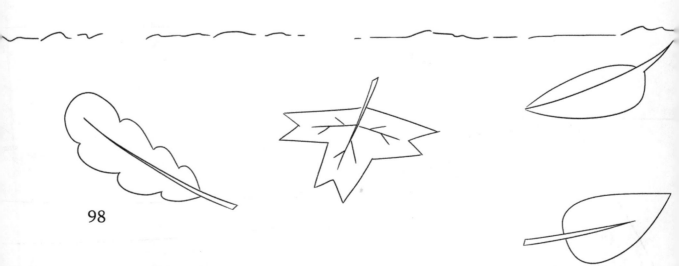

Tiptoeing

When you tiptoe across the floor,
Is the floor less creaky than before?
When you tiptoe over dry ground,
Do leaves not make a *crunch!* sound?
When you tiptoe from here to there,
Do your feet become lighter than air?
Is tiptoeing quieter night and day,
Or should you just walk the entire way?

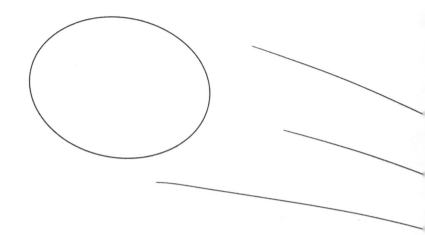

Thar He Blows!

When Grandpa Lows blows his nose,
It sounds like exploding torpedoes,
Or great cannonballs in the sky,
That go *caboom!* way up high.
When Grandpa Lows puts a tissue to his nose,
We all close our ears and scream, "Thar he blows!"

Babies

When babies are born, they look like a storm.
From chimpanzees to chickadees,
It seems to be nature's norm.
Animal, bird, and human babies of all kinds
Are born wobbly and scraggly,
And, gosh, nearly blind!
Babies cry at the drop of a dime.
They crawl and fall and can't talk at all.
If being a kid is hard, try being a baby sometime!

Happy Harry

Happy Harry knew how to be merry.
He celebrated a sweet cherry.
He saluted as the splendid sun rose.
He playfully plucked a pretty rose.
The simplest, everyday things
Were lucky breaks for him.
His well of joy never ran dry.
He never asked when or why.
Happy Harry accepted his lot
And he almost never forgot
To thank the finer and lesser things
That always had Happy Harry rejoicing.

Pound Cake

Kate had one pound of eggs,
One pound of sugar,
One pound of butter,
And one pound of flour.
She mixed them up,
And within the hour,
She had four pounds of cake!
She ate four pounds of what she baked,
And within two days,
She gained ten pounds of weight.
It was all because she ate
One pound of eggs,
One pound of sugar,
One pound of butter,
And one pound of flour!

School of Hard Knocks

It would be pretty cool
To have three months of school.
We'd surely be blessed
With vacation for the rest.
We'd exchange our comfy desks
For afternoons in the wilderness.
We'd give up our science books
For fishing lines and bait hooks.
We'd learn a whole lot
From the school of hard knocks.
But what we learn from the school of life
Wouldn't be nearly as nice!

Gift Bows

Sue's gift seemed wrapped in heaven.
It had golden bows—no less than seven!
The tower of presents was tied with ribbon.
Sue gasped at the gift she was given.
It looked too pretty for Sue to open.
So, for years, it sat in the kitchen.
Ten years passed, and Sue at last
Thought it best to sneak a peek.
She held the wrapped gift close to her heart,
Untied the bows and was off to a good start.
She looked inside to find an old ham.
She held her nose at the shriveled Spam.
Sue fancied the bow and its golden glow.
So, she threw out the ham and kept the bow!

Two Bodies

Brody said, "I want to be somebody."
Erin said, "But you are somebody."
Brody said, "No. I don't want to be just anybody."
Erin said, "But you are Brody to everybody!"
Brody said, "Nah. I'm just a nobody."
And that's how it went between two bodies!

Remembering

I forgot something. I don't know what.
But I remembered that I forgot.
I just can't think of what I forgot.
Seems I remembered that I've forgotten what I forgot!

Extra Careful

Willy Wilbul was extra careful.
He did everything to stay out of harm's way.
He sanitized his room each and every day.
If there was a sick neighbor on his floor,
To keep the germs out, he bolted his door.
He wiped down his phone after every call.
He uncluttered the floor so he wouldn't fall.
Every hour, he washed his hands with soap.
When a friend asked him out, he said nope!
One surprising day, he went out on a whim.
As careful Willy Wilbul walked down the street,
A bed slipped out of a window and fell on him!

Proper

Roger Ropper is very proper.
He eats ham sandwiches with a fork and knife.
He's the most proper man you'll see in your life.
He won't reach across the table for the butter.
He won't burp, slouch, gossip, or mutter.
He holds the door open for ladies and gents,
Even if that meant . . .
He'd have to wait still as a statue,
To let the long line of folks pass through!

Getting By

It's a fact of life that you can get by
Without giving some things a try,
Like cans of Spam
(that never-expiring ham!),
Or Auntie Em's fruitcakes,
And unfrosted corn flakes,
Or the mistletoe above my head,
And that gross kiss from Winifred.
There are some things, flat out,
That a kid can do without!

Fargo

Wilson Filly lived in a town called Fargo.
There, temperatures dropped to twenty below.
The winters were so chilly,
It bothered Wilson Filly.
To make up for the cold weather,
Wilson decided to put together
Something tropical and nice
That wouldn't feel cold as ice.
He planted palm trees indoors
And lined coconuts across the floors.
He built a box and filled it with sand.
He made tropical stir-fry in a frying pan.
He wore shorts, sunglasses, and a hat
And sat on a chair on his living room mat.
In Fargo, Wilson Filly still feels the chill,
But his beachy setup makes up for the heating bill!

Doing It All

Chester McMall thought he could do it all.
He rode his bike while fishing.
He ate pea soup while whistling.
He did magic tricks while fixing his bike,
And mixed lemonade while holding his mic.
Of course, the fish didn't bite.
The soup flew everywhere, all right.
His bike never got fixed,
And the lemonade wasn't mixed.
Doing it all at once seemed a great feat,
But as it turned out, nothing was complete.
With his hands in a bit of everything,
Chester ended up not doing anything!

Leaf Polish

Gardener Gail polishes the leaves of her plants.
She says it keeps away the spiders and ants.
After she's polished each leaf and petal,
The shiny, live plant looks artificial!

Givers

We're all givers and sometimes takers.
We can be fighters or peacemakers.
Each of us has something to give.
And we all help each other live.
Granny bakes fresh pecan tarts.
Kyle shares Valentine's Day hearts.
Dr. Dave fixes your broken bone.
Neighbor Sam flies her rotor drone.
Jay tells jokes that make you laugh.
Zookeeper Dan cares for the giraffe.
If there's ever a giver that I missed,
Just add her to *your* great giver list!
There are enough givers in town
To make the world go 'round!

Expiration Dates

Things ought to have an expiration date,
Not only eggs and milk,
But also anger and hate.
Toss out the hate when it starts to stink.
Throw out the anger when it turns sour.
You can't keep things that will spoil
Your mood, your day, or your hour!

Juggelyrunch

I've munched on a juggelyrunch!
Seems I can't chew or crunch!
It's stuck between my teeth.
Oh me, oh my!
I can't drink or eat or speak!
Now my mouth won't open,
'Cause of the juggelyrunch I've eaten!

Princess

Anna Lou was born in Kathmandu.
Harry and Grace adopted this little girl
And gave her the best life in the world.
Anna Lou played with ponies and dolls.
She even traveled to Niagara Falls.
Still, Anna Lou was glum,
Glum as a wrinkly sugar plum.
Then one fine summer afternoon, Anna Lou
Found out she was born a princess in Kathmandu!
She had smiled nonstop ever since that day.
Princess Anna Lou was cheerful as a sunshine ray.
Everything else stayed the same.
The only difference was her name!

Long Drive

Ed went for a drive to clear his mind.
He went for such a long drive
That by the time he got back,
His mind had nothing left inside!

Waiting for Success

Ten-year-old Miko said cheerily,
"Success will come to me."
He waited and waited, and it wasn't to be.
Then Miko turned twenty-three.
Everyone said, "Make your own success."
But Miko disagreed.
He replied, "Success is destined for me."
Miko eventually turned fifty-three.
At middle age, he yearned to see
The success he thought was meant to be.
"Create your success," they all said eagerly.
But Miko wouldn't listen, saying,
"Success will come ultimately."
Miko celebrated eighty-three.
For success, he held on patiently.
Then Miko went to heaven.
Up in the clouds, we could all see
Miko still waiting for success posthumously.

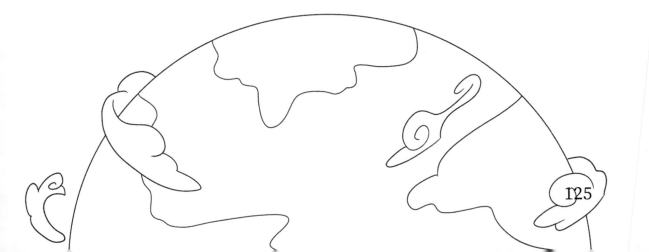

Cloud Storage

Nana asked Pedro for his homework.
He said that it's saved in the cloud.
His nana started to yell loud,
"It's saved in the cloud? The cloud?
Pedro, if we have a dust storm,
Your homework will blow a mile high!
If we have a thunderstorm,
Your homework will become wet as rain!
If we have a hailstorm,
Your homework will be torn apart!
If we have a windstorm,
Your homework will gust to the next town!
Pedro, get your homework off the cloud."
Pedro thought and replied,
"Nana, it's a nice day. It'll be all right."

Disappointed

Dexter the Expecter
Expected a lot of things.
He expected a punctual train.
For his lettuce, he expected romaine.
He expected lucky breaks.
He expected unburnt cakes.
Then Dexter started to expect
Something called respect.
He expected heaps of praise.
At work, he expected a big raise.
He expected laughter at his jokes.
He expected applause from all folks.
Dexter the Expecter expected a whole lot.
But most of what he expected, he just never got.
Because Dexter the Expecter always expected,
Most of the time, he was just disappointed!

Kevin the Planner

Kevin Spanner was a planner.
He made great plans of all sorts,
In every way, and in every manner.
But his marvelous plans never stuck.
He'd twist 'em and fold 'em,
Nail 'em and hammer 'em, hoping for luck.
Kevin's plans always broke in two,
Or, they'd melt, crash, or fall apart.
They never turned out as he expected them to.
Kevin no longer makes plans of any kind.
Now carefree, he blows with the wind.
Wherever it goes, he's happy not to mind!

Inside and Outside

Some people suppose that . . .
If you dress nice on the outside,
You're just as nice on the inside.

Other people suppose that . . .
If you dress sloppy on the outside,
You're just as messy on the inside.

What people don't know is that . . .
It doesn't matter if you dress sloppy or smart.
All that matters is that you've got a nice (though messy) heart!

Irresponsible

Dilbert Dribble wasn't responsible.
When he slipped on the ice
And dropped the cupcake tree,
He sourly blamed the bakery.
When he leaned on the hot stove
And scorched his fuzzy goatee,
He cursed the appliance company.
When he crashed his boat onto the beach
And explained that the sea belched out the shore,
It wasn't much too long before
Dilbert Dribble was finally held responsible.

Little Bess

Little Bess is a mess.
She plucked herself bare,
Since no one seemed to care.
She wanted a feathered friend,
A parrot who'd stay 'til the end.
But in her closed cage, she lived alone.
So, she plucked her feathers to the bone.
Next time you meet a lonely bird, like Little Bess,
Send her love, so she won't pluck herself featherless.

Smallest Town in the World

The town of Hum in Croatia is really small.
It has a population of twenty-five people in all.
There are two narrow streets where
You'll find one restaurant and one square.
Everyone knows the policeman and the baker,
The shop owner, the teacher, and the mayor.
Your school probably has more boys and girls
Than the smallest town in the world!

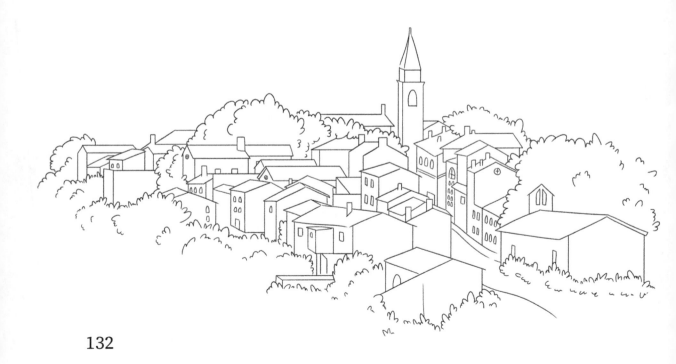

Halfsome

"Would you like some wholesome bread?" asked Baker Jim.
"I'd like some halfsome, please," answered Teng Ting,
"Because I'm too small to eat the whole wholesome thing!"

134

Envy

Envy is a creepy, crawly bug
That thinks it's some kind of thug.
When it grows big, it gets really bad.
It reminds me of things I never had,
Like Mike's incredible skateboard
Or Samurai Akio's fighting sword.
When it gains muscle, it beats me up.
Envy makes me think I'm not good enough.
It forces me to want more than I've got.
Envy sure bothers me a whole lot!
So, I got smart and shut the door,
Never to let envy in anymore.

Nothing's Certain

If there's one thing in life that Ben knew was certain,
It's that he never knew what was going to happen.
He could be struck by a bolt of lightning,
Or win a prize for Boogaloo dancing.
He could tumble on a slippery sidewalk,
Or get hee-haws for a funny jibbleejauk.
His kite might get stuck in a tree,
Or he might win the lottery.
Ben never knew what was in store.
But it would sure make things different than before!

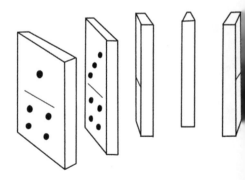

Anything Goes

Anything goes, said old Mr. Boze,
From snow-white crows
To the awkward selfie pose,
Or the neighbor who blows
His nose right into his clothes,
From madcaps who chose
To chase whirling tornadoes,
To creepy, evening shadows
That bring the days to a close,
Or tuxedoed cowboys at rodeos
And perfectly falling dominoes.
Strange things are always those
That startle you out of your doze.

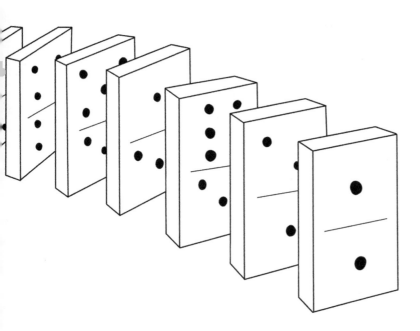

Carefree

How nice it must be
To be so carefree.
To ride a bike in the wind
To hike around the bend
To camp out at night
To gaze at stars so bright
To roast marshmallows for s'mores
To jump in puddles when it pours
To catch fireflies in late June
To dream of flying to the moon
To eat snow cones (three too many)
To not worry about a single penny.
Now that I've turned eighty,
These things just won't be.
I sure had my day.
Now it's yours today.
Go on, kid, go and play!

Friendly Miss Brenda Dunn

Miss Brenda Dunn was a friend to everyone,
From the gal at the deli to the stranger in the tree.
Since Miss Brenda Dunn didn't practice caution,
She had to build a ten-foot fence around her mansion!

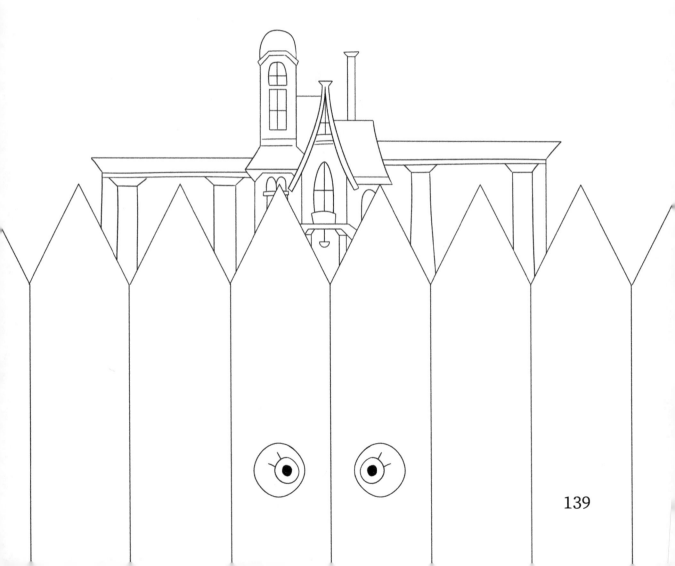

Sports

Raina was no know-it-all, so she asked Randall,
"What's it called when you hit a ball,
Run around a diamond, and don't fall?"
Randall said, "That's called baseball."

Raina, once again, asked Randall,
"What's it called when you throw a ball
Into a basket and the referee makes a travel call?"
Randall said, "That's called basketball."

Raina asked a third question, this time to Randolph.
"What's it called when you hit a ball
After shimmying and getting your hips to bop?"
"Oh," said Randolph, "that's called golf."

Life Manual

There's no life manual or book
That teaches a kid how . . .
To tie shoelaces
Or make funny faces
To make porridge taste good
Or make you feel understood
To draw hopscotch grids
Or close uncloseable lids
To drink from the hose
Or wiggle all ten toes
To color outside the lines
Or avoid library fines
To care for a pet goldfish
Or make a birthday wish
To dance in moonbeams
Or find funny memes
To look on the bright side
Or know where to hide.
But kids do these things anyway,
In their own special way.
Now and then, they learn to know,
And really, that's how kids grow!

Friend

Sam was looking for a friend,
Someone who'll . . .
Meet her halfway and around the bend,
Write her a card though there's an email to send,
Help her chipped heart start to mend,
Give her love instead of just lend,
And always, always . . .
Hear what she said but know what she meant.

Different

Paul is different,
Different than the rest.
It doesn't mean he's the worst.
It doesn't mean he's the best.
It doesn't put him first.
It doesn't put him last.
It doesn't make him slow.
It doesn't make him fast.
He's just different, though.
He's not strange
. . . or weird.
He's not sad
. . . or feared.
He's just different than the rest.
But he's as different as everyone else!

Words

Kay spotted a spotted ladybug.
It crawled across her coffee mug.
She crossed her T's in a letter.
She steeped her tea 'til it was bitter.
She dotted her I's in a note.
She lost her glass eye in a boat.
Now she can't see to finish this rhyme.
So, she'll stay at sea 'til the end of time.

I Ain't No Tree

I was in the kitchen when
I heard a high-pitched musical sound.
So, I twirled my wonderin' head around.
I spied a grasshopper on the wall.
It made a chirpy kind of call.
It looked me right in the eye.
I was startled and walked on by.
It was just a speck but jumped on my neck.
I said, "I ain't no tree!" and gave a shout.
"My neck is not bark! It won't sprout!"
I gave it a flick and off my neck it skipped.
It disappeared into a nearby houseplant.
I never saw it again. But I heard it rant.
It sang about a tree.
But grasshopper, that ain't me.

Collector of Things

My brother is a collector of things,
From stamps and coins to books and springs.
He enjoys the cheer his collection brings.

His stamps are old, faded, and torn.
They're worth more if they're not worn.
His coins come from faraway lands,
From Spain and Greece to South Sudan!
The pages of his books are crisp and new.
He won't let me read them, in case I achoo!
His springs are slinky and lay in the hall.
If I trip over one, I just might fall!

Now that my brother is older,
His collection has grown bolder.
It certainly won't fit neatly in a folder.

He now collects animals, like wild cats.
Up in the rafters, I've even seen bats!
The elephant in the backyard is the best;
He's bigger and gentler than the rest.
The ostrich keeps her head in the ground.
It's as if she wants no one around.
The kangaroo jumps over the fence in the yard.
The neighbors get mad, but I laugh really hard!

Our days are never a bore.
Spotted leopards freely roar,
And anteaters loudly snore!

Once, his collection was on the news.
Out came news people and TV crews.
My brother's sloth had escaped,
Last seen behind the drapes.
It had crept into the neighbor's chair,
Then into a drawer of underwear!
Mr. Fred ran out of his house,
Screaming about a giant mouse!

Of all the things my brother might collect,
From old clocks to wax insects,
I never know what to expect!

His collection has made our house a zoo!
I started charging visitors a dollar or two.
I made a nice sum by the end of the day,
As people lined up from far, far away.
Talk of his collection spread around.
Now my kid brother is famous in town.
It all started when he collected things,
From stamps to the pink flamingo that sings.

His animal collection is his newest yet.
They're the goofiest creatures I've ever met.
I dare not guess what he'll collect next!

Thank you for reading *Collector of Things & Other Poems*! If these poems gave you a chuckle, please consider leaving a review!

Children's books by Riya Aarini
Cole and the Giant Gingerbread House
The Veggie Patch Bandits
Pickerton's Jiggle
Ollie's Garden
Ollie's Haffiness
Upcoming children's books by Riya Aarini
The Country Bake-Off

Stay up to date on new children's book releases by visiting
www.riyapresents.com.

Index

CPSIA information can be obtained
at www.ICGtesting.com
Printed in the USA
LVHW101758160821
695429LV00011B/281